George Duffield

A Thanksgiving Discourse

The Rule of Divine Providence applicable to the present circumstances of

our country, delivered in the First Presbyterian church of Detroit,

Thursday, November 28, 1860

George Duffield

A Thanksgiving Discourse
The Rule of Divine Providence applicable to the present circumstances of our country, delivered in the First Presbyterian church of Detroit, Thursday, November 28, 1860

ISBN/EAN: 9783337234621

Printed in Europe, USA, Canada, Australia, Japan

Cover: Foto ©Andreas Hilbeck / pixelio.de

More available books at **www.hansebooks.com**

A THANKSGIVING DISCOURSE.

THE

RULE OF DIVINE PROVIDENCE

APPLICABLE TO THE

PRESENT CIRCUMSTANCES OF OUR COUNTRY.

DELIVERED IN THE

FIRST PRESBYTERIAN CHURCH OF DETROIT,

Thursday, November 28, 1860.

BY GEO. DUFFIELD.

DETROIT:
FREE PRESS MAMMOTH BOOK AND JOB PRINTING HOUSE
1861.

CORRESPONDENCE.

DETROIT, January 19, 1861.

To THE REV. GEO. DUFFIELD,

        DEAR SIR:

                Having listened with pleasure to your discourse, prepared and delivered on the National Fast Day, and being of the opinion that many of the facts and suggestions therein contained, and much of the counsel affected by it might prove of service, if more generally circulated through the community, we beg leave to ask of you a copy of the same for publication.

Those of the undersigned, who likewise enjoyed the privilege of listening to your Thanksgiving Sermon in November last, would be pleased to have a copy of that also, in order that the two might be jointly published.

We remain, with much respect,
Your obedient servants,

H. H. WELLS,	D. COOPER,
HENRY A. MORROW,	J. W. TILLMAN,
GEO. W. HOFFMAN,	J. A. FARRELL,
N. MINER PRATT,	J. S. FARRAND,
C. N. GANSON,	A. KNIGHT,
C. H. BUHL,	W. S. PENFIELD,
J. W. BAGLEY,	MORSE STUART,
C. M. DAVISON,	C. VAN HUSAN,
F. J. DOUGALL,	GEO. S. FROST.

DETROIT, January 26, 1861.

To H. H. WELLS, HENRY A. MORROW,

    GEO. W. HOFFMAN, J. W. TILLMAN, AND OTHERS:

GENTLEMEN:

           In the hope you inspire, that the discourses of which you request copies, "might prove of service, if more generally circulated through the community," it gives me pleasure to comply with your request.

With much respect and Christian regard,

I remain, yours, truly,

GEO. DUFFIELD.

THANKSGIVING DISCOURSE.

JERE. 18: 7, 8. "At what instant I shall speak concerning a nation and concerning a kingdom, to pluck up, and to pull down, and to destroy it; if that nation, against whom I have pronounced, turn from their evil, I will repent of the evil that I thought to do unto them."

OUR annual day of Thanksgiving meets us under circumstances so strongly marked, and of such striking contrast, as to bid us "rejoice with fear and trembling." Seldom has there been a year so crowned with the goodness of the Lord, in many respects, as the past. "His paths have dropped fatness," and "the little hills have rejoiced on every side." Abundant, exuberant crops have poured plenty into the lap of the husbandman; the fruits of the earth have been reaped and gathered, and stored in richest profusion; commerce and trade had recovered from the embarrassments and distrust, for a year or two previous, so prevalent and perplexing; no pestilence has invaded our cities, nor disease of mortal malignity prostrated any wide extent of our country; nor epidemic any limited district. The seasons have been marked with health, and unusually exempt from extreme degrees of heat or cold, or sudden and violent fluctuations. Tempests and tornadoes, floods and flames, have accomplished less than ordinary destruction. The ravages of death have been more than ordinarily restrained. The mortality of our city has been much less than usual, and no conflagration, or calamity of a public nature, has filled our habitations with sorrow. Although sad and painful calamities have here and there occurred, and we have been called, as a congregation, to mourn with parents whose hearts were broken by the untimely loss of a beloved and promising son; yet much fewer than in previous years, have been the visits required from us to the city of the dead. And although here and there, in the southern portions of our land, the showers of heaven have been withheld, the verdant field turned into a dry and barren waste, and the hideous spectre of famine reared her frightful form in some of our distant borders, yet has there been more than abundance to meet the deficiency of provender and provisions thus caused, and a prompt exercise of generous liberality, to prevent and mitigate the threatened suffering. "The pastures have been clothed with flocks, the valleys, also, have been covered over with corn," and the shout of joy, and the song of praise, have ascended from nearly every corner of our land.

Amid these tokens of unmerited goodness, however, are to be seen indications of a fearful and portentous nature. It has been a year of religious declension. But few revivals of religion have blessed the churches. The zeal and prayerfulness of many have subsided into monotonous formality. "The solemn feasts" and Sabbaths have by many been forgot-

ten. The sanctuaries of the Lord have been dese-
crated; few have come to the solemn assemblies. Vice
and immorality, in various forms, are on the increase;
intemperance laughs at the restraints of the law;
public opinion sustains not its enforcement; professors of religion extensively frown upon and condemn
attempts for that purpose. The Sabbath has become
a day of traffic, of sensual indulgence, and of noisy
amusement, and drunken excesses and brawls; and
places of corruption, whirlpools of perdition, spring
up around, while magistrates, ministers of justice and
law, and multitudes that name the name of Christ,
rest at ease, and consent and "love to have it so."
Party political strifes have greatly neutralized christian influence. The wicked have walked on every
side, and vile and unprincipled men have been ex-
alted, by catering to the corrupt passions and de-
praved appetites of the lovers of strong drink. Nothing, comparatively worth speaking of, is done to stay
the tide of intemperance and of Sabbath desecration,
which are sweeping so many of our youth and others to the drunkard's grave. God's gifts have been
abused. His mercies have been despised or forgot-
ten. "Dumb dogs, that cannot bark," have stood as
sentinels of the press; and the work of corruption,
the ravages of intemperance, the increase of crime,
move forward without molestation, or hindrance of
any great efficiency from officers of justice, churches
of the living God, and christian professors generally.

These are alarming requitals for the goodness and
mercy and loving kindness of the Lord. Suddenly,
and most unexpectedly, in the midst of abundance,

a cloud of gloom and darkness overspreads the sky. Extraordinary dispensations of Providence excite alarming apprehensions. The bonds of Union, that have for nearly three-fourths of a century held us united as a confederate government of free and independent States, become relaxed, and threats of severance and separation are heard. A panic in the commercial world produces dismay; State securities and stocks of every sort are depreciated; an inflated currency excites distrust; business and trade have become stagnant; embarrassments are thrown in the way of forwarding our abundant crops to market; exchange, for a season, is rendered almost impracticable; the Lord has blown upon men's anticipated gains, and "he that earneth wages, earneth wages to put it into a bag with holes." Consternation seizes the wise and the wary; confusion takes the place of confidence; and the providence of God is heard to "*speak concerning the nation*" and government, not as it was hoped it would, to plant and prosper, but "to pluck up, and to pull down, and to destroy."

It behooves us, on such an occasion as the present—met as we are to render thanks to God for mercies abounding—to ponder also, and seek to profit from judgments impending. God, in a season of prosperity, security and increasing sinful provocation, has suddenly given warning of approaching judgments. He thus calls to repentance and reformation. If they are not so improved, men may please themselves with hopes of deliverance or safety, and think, by their wisdom and skill, to prevent or counteract threatened ills; but the wisdom of the wise will be found foolishness, and the resources of the mighty utterly weak and unavailing. There is but one way of averting the Divine displeasure, and escaping from impending judgment; that is, repentance and reformation. "If the nation," saith God, "against whom I have pronounced, turn from their evil, I will repent of the evil that I thought to do unto them." Such is THE RULE OF HIS RIGHTEOUS PROVIDENCE. We invite your attention to it AS APPLICABLE TO THE PRESENT CIRCUMSTANCES OF OUR COUNTRY.

I. The rule itself becomes a righteous God, in His government of the world. There is, in the minds of men, an inward sense of right— a deep and abiding conviction—that they should suffer, who, having been previously warned, will not repent of their sins. It is not necessary that one man teach this to another. It is inseparable from our intelligent nature. Every man intuitively feels, in his own conscious convictions, with respect to himself and others, that impenitent sinners, incurable by divine warning, are proper objects of the divine displeasure. Impunity, under such circumstances, would prove a great temptation to atheism. It is right and becoming, therefore, that God, in His own time and way, should vindicate His faithfulness, by executing His threatenings. For, if men can at any time banish the fear and restraint of impending judgments, and persuade themselves there is no danger of coming wrath, no God that judgeth righteously on the earth, there is nothing too vile, dishonest, profane and flagitious, they will not eventually consent to and commit. "Because sentence against an evil work is not speedily executed, therefore the heart of the sons of men is fully set in them to do evil."

It is with nations as with individuals; long continued prosperity, and escape from threatened and impending judgments, amid growing vice and immorality, tend to hardness of heart, profligacy of life, imperious oppression, increasing corruption, and provocations of crime. Those that love and fear God, who prize His gospel, and seek to do right, instinctively cry to Him for redress, deliverance, and safety, when provoking sins and abounding crimes prevail. The Spirit leads them thus to pray, and God has promised to hear their prayer. Should iniquity always triumph, and impunity in this world always accompany provoking crimes and a corrupt administration of government, the temptation would be too strong for the faith of weak believers. Hence the interpositions of severe and sudden wrath, occasionally, by signal and righteous judgment, where warnings and impending evils have not produced repentance and reformation. It is right and becoming in a holy God, who has said He will "avenge His elect that cry unto Him day and night," thus to vindicate His faithfulness and glory.

II. In applying this rule to the circumstances of our own country, there are several inquiries of importance for us successively to consider; and,

First. What indications are there of iniquities so abounding, and of judgments so impending, as to call for speedy repentance in order to escape greater evils? As to the first part of this inquiry, we remark, that there is no need for us to enter into a specific enumeration of all sorts of crimes, in their varieties, observable at this day in our country. We may differ also from others and many, in our estimate of particular vices in society. It will be sufficient, briefly, to state a few things, which, the sacred Scriptures teach us, indicate a corrupt state of society, requiring repentance and reformation for deliverance from impending judgments.

1. The first is, when all sorts of crimes are on the increase. Such a state of things indicates a general corrupt state of society, like that of the prophet referred to in Israel, when he lamented, " Ah, sinful nation, a people laden with iniquity, a seed of evil-doers, children that are corrupters, they have forsaken the Lord; they have provoked the Holy One of Israel to anger; they have gone away backward."* That vice and immorality are on the increase in our land, none can deny. The statistics of crime, the columns of the daily gazettes, prove it. It is not designed to intimate, that, as a people, we are as corrupt as are other nations which might be named, or as we may yet become without repentance and reformation. But there are few provoking sins condemned in the word of God, and known to be worthy of punishment by man as well as God, that are not to be found in the catalogue of our guilt as a people. From the most impudent and law-defying atheism—that has attempted to impose upon the common sense of the communities in our

---

* Isaiah 1: 5.

large cities, especially New York, by claiming the protection of our federal constitution for theatrical exhibitions, and musical concerts, and lager beer festivals on the Sabbath, in open defiance of municipal law and public sentiment, under the blasphemous pretext of these things being their worship and their rights of conscience—down through the vilest intemperance, sensuality and uncleanness, to every phase of dishonesty, deception, oppression, and moral degradation, may we trace the black and odious list. Who will dare to make it a plea with God on our behalf, that we are free from prevalent profanity, horrid oaths and blasphemies, open and wanton desecration of the Sabbath, filial disobedience, contempt of parental authority, bloodshed, murder, drunkenness, licentiousness, lewdness, repudiation of marriage contracts, adultery, theft, burglary, swindling, wholesale fraud and gambling of every hateful sort, oppression, slavery, with all its catalogue of abominations, falsehood and defamation of every type, and avarice with its endless cruelties and exactions? Not one. Not only have these sins a growing prevalence, indicating a corrupt state of society, but a second indication of this observable is, that:

2. All sorts of persons, and every grade of society, are involved in them; many by their own personal guilt; still more by not doing what they can to prevent them in others. All sorts of persons, in every profession and vocation, are found consenting to the relaxation of law, and to the venality of officers of government. The proof of this is to be seen; in elevating corrupt men to places of trust and power; in

not testifying openly and publicly against the vices prevalent; in indifference and refusal to adopt and co-operate in measures for the execution of law; and in not mourning for what they cannot remedy. And not only is the world around full of such sins as are its own, appropriate to men of unbelieving minds, and unrenewed by the spirit of holiness. But,

3. A third characteristic is, that churches, and professors of religion extensively, are not free from a participation in them, but practice such as are peculiar to them—pride, vanity, boasting, ostentation, self-righteousness, luxury, covetousness, ambition, sensuality, conformity to corrupt fashions, and drinking usages, formality, deadness and coldness in religion, indifference to the cause of God, the claims of the Sabbath, and public morals, rivalry, proselytism, want of cordial co-operation, self-applause, loss of zeal for God and Christ, seeking their own ease, hypocrisy, and making religion often a cloak for unrighteousness, or a stepping-stone to commercial, political, or social ambitious preferment. These things are so obvious, that all the fair glosses of a mere profession of religion cannot conceal them. Thus is Christ wounded in the house of His friends; and many of the wicked stumble, and find occasion to reproach and blaspheme, and proclaim themselves skeptical and devoid of confidence altogether in relation to real vital godliness. Certainly such things call for repentance, and cannot be sufficiently bewailed. Sad evidence is there, not only that the foolish, but that all the virgins, wise and foolish, slumber and sleep while the Lord delayeth His coming.

4. Beside these, we may discern indications, that, in some respects, our sins, more strictly national, are becoming more than ordinarily aggravated, and that in despite of solemn warning. Intemperance has been, and yet is, one of our national sins. It has been fearfully rebuked by the annual immolation of 100,000 of our fellow citizens, by the steady increase of onerous taxes, by crowded jails and poor houses, by the multiplication of the insane, by demands for lunatic and drunkards' and other asylums, and by the lawlessness, and murders, and other crimes it produces. Yet public opinion treats it as a matter of indifference; will not sanction and call for the enforcement of the prohibitory liquor law; elevates to office men that treat it with contempt; sustains and justifies public functionaries sworn to enforce the laws, who perjure themselves by not doing it; looks, with allowance and approbation, upon the conspiracy of liquor dealers to defy the law and tread down the Sabbath; and countenances the vending and use of adulterated and poisonous mixtures, known, and publicly proved, to be abominable and murderous frauds practiced on the community. With all the clear light upon this subject, and the numerous rebukes, which God in his providence administers for this sin, it is no small aggravation of our guilt, that such a state of things, on the part of rulers and ruled, should continue.

Another of our great national sins, becoming more and more aggravated, is the growing practical contempt for the moral obligation of concontracts. The federal government violated the faith of its treaties with the Cherokee Indians. Official oaths are extensively disregarded. A man's word in business, especially his promise, was once extensively regarded as good as his bond. Honor and honesty were safeguards of social compacts. But now, no man regards himself safe from imposition and unfaithfulness to promises and contracts, except in so far as he can vindicate his claims and rights by process of law. Even securities, given according to law, for the faithful performance of official duties, or in private contracts, are regarded as worthless, and laughed at both in the church and in the world. Subscriptions, on the part both of religious professors and irreligious men, even when expressed in promissory notes, are repudiated without shame and compunction. Men accept of places of trust, and ridicule the idea of their being required or expected faithfully to discharge their duties. Stations of influence, places of power and patronage are sought, not for the public good, but for personal advantage. Covenant engagements, and the duties thence arising, even among church members, are esteemed but light affairs, relinquishable at will. Religious professors, in managing voluntary societies, and religious associations and congregations, under various pretexts, pervert funds, alienate property, and set examples of robbery and fraud, allied to the swindling operations of unprincipled men in banks, and other corporate companies. The provisions of Federal and State constitutions are disregarded; and Legislative enactments and judiciary decisions are framed to render them worthless. Honest, confiding, conscientious, order-loving and law-abiding citizens, are betrayed and robbed by the promises and schemes of speculators. One generation begins to sneer at the idea of compacts being binding on them, which have descended from a former. The son repudiates the obligations of the father. Many repudiate their own, and fail, or make assignments, after having covered up whatever property they can conceal, and eventually are found to have purchased their own notes at heavy discounts, and defrauded their creditors. "Judgment is fallen in the streets, and equity cannot enter." The very ligaments of the social state are sundered. Even the marriage compact begins to be regarded by many as binding only as long as convenient.

Another of our great national sins beginning to develop itself is the avaricious pursuit of gain. Commercial greatness is the idol and ambition of all our chief cities. Desire for wealth, in rapid and large accumulation, renders many ready to prey, each upon his neighbor, and laugh at the idea of honor or honesty in commercial transactions, beyond the flagrant offenses which can be detected and punished at law. It is becoming characteristic of us, as a people, to sacrifice time, social and domestic comfort, and to neglect the means of moral and religious improvement, in the mad and hot pursuit of wealth. Nothing but amusement attracts the masses; science and religion have but few votaries that can give an evening or two a week for improvement. God has rebuked this spirit, again and again, by the embarrassments of trade, the revulsions in the market, the panics started, the depreciation of stocks and property, and the destruction of confidence and credit in business. Yet no change, no repentance, no reformation takes place, but the absorption of mind and heart, and the rush, are as great as ever, and greater, after extravagant profits and illicit gain, whenever the pressure of impending judgment is lightened. After repeated warnings, such things greatly aggravate the guilt of that "covetousness which is idolatry."

It is scarcely necessary to add, that slavery, with its accompaniments and consequents, is another of our great national evils and God-provoking sins. But the violence of party strife, the alienations and rivalries, the jealousies, and fears, and reproaches, and collisions of interest between those involved in it and those relatively affected by it, and the contests for political victory, in the absence of moral influence and fraternal sympathy and good will, have thrown far back, apparently, the day of repentance and reformation. Passion has taken the place of reason. Prejudice has overpowered conscience. Christianity has been invoked to subsidize oppression. Churches have been rent. Alienations have been rendered apparently incurable, and loud threats are heard of secession, separation, and dissolution of the Union. These things are omens of dread import, and they suggest a second leading inquiry:

Second. What are the ordinary impending judgments, foretokening approaching crises of distress, calamity or ruin, and which can only be prevented

2

by repentance? Judgments, as we learn from the sacred Scriptures, are either of a temporal or spiritual nature. Of the former, are seasons of affliction, wide-spread disease, especially visitations of pestilence, seasons of want and privation, when the Lord turns His hand upon men's gains, withers their crops, blasts their fields, destroys their business, and renders their labor and industry unproductive and valueless. A third method is when He sends the ravages of mildew and various insects, droughts, floods, tempests, tornadoes and such like, that cause suffering and famine to a greater or less extent. A fourth is, when He lets loose the restraints of His providence, and allows assaults and injuries and fell passions prevailing, to lead to war. Another method is to make rulers a curse, and cause the people to suffer from mercenary cruelty and oppression by ruinous policy adopted, or utter recklessness and profligacy, and infidelity in the execution of their trust and responsibilities. And still another and disastrous method is, to inflict spiritual judgments, by withholding His Holy Spirit, so that the churches, becoming cold and dead, corrupt, and copying the fashions of the world, make a profession of religion such a formal, hypocritical thing, that it loses all its moral power and redeeming influence.

All these things are tokens of the divine displeasure. Whenever and wherever they occur, loud are the calls of God to immediate repentance. We need not say, that in retracing the history of the past sixty years, we can discern all these things to have occurred among ourselves. Seasons of agricultural, manufacturing and commercial prosperity, through years of general health, have been followed with seasons of disease, commercial disaster, visitations in different forms of pestilence, partial famines, war, and general anxiety and distress. Seasons of great and extensive revival and religious awakening, have been succeeded by those of stupor, worldliness, sensuality and selfishness, awakening the uneasy fears of watchmen stationed on the walls of the church, and others seeking the honor of God and the salvation of men.

Divine Providence has afflicted us as a people in the most marked manner, again and again; and the present money panic, in the midst of abundance and animating prospects of commercial prosperity—occurring in a day of religious declension, and immediately consequent on political contests and jubilations— seems to be the very voice of God, proclaiming His displeasure, and calling to repentance. We may think, and say, that it has been unnecessary, and refer it to this cause and the other; to political intrigues, or the rage of disappointed partisans, or cupidity of scheming speculators; and we may say, as we read the movements of Providence, that they who have sown the wind, are reaping the whirlwind. But the fact is not to be questioned, that suddenly, as by the violent jerk of a powerful bit in the jaws, the prancing fiery steed has been reined in, and made almost to fall, so has the commercial world been arrested, and made for a moment to stand amazed and tremble. It is the call of God: "Repent, and turn yourselves from all your transgressions, so that your iniquity does not prove your ruin." Warning after warning has been given—rebuke after rebuke, and now, unexpectedly, in rapid succession, in the midst of rejoicings, and when least expected, it is repeated, as though some fearful crisis in Providence is at hand.

What that crisis is, is obvious to every intelligent observer of passing events. It is the dissolution of the Union, that binds together in harmony and prosperity this great confederacy of free and independent States. Such an event could not fail to produce results in every respect to be deprecated, if not fatally disastrous to the future well-being of these United States, severally as well as collectively. The history of the revolution, and of the trials and frequent agony of the great father of his country, raised up and sustained so wonderfully by a gracious Providence, during the years of contest with Great Britain, proved the perils and perplexities of a mere States' compact and legislative council, which formed the bond of union among associated colonies, or brought men together by pressing exigencies. The federal constitution, framed with so much care and wisdom by the great patriots and statesmen assembled in convention in 1787—the names of many of whom emblazon the annals of our country's fame,—and adopted successively, with amendments, suggested by different individual States, became a bond of union of such enhanced force and aptitude, that when consummated by the organization of a federal government, was thought and proclaimed by multitudes to be perpetual and indisso-

luble. It has been the element of our greatness
and glory as a free and independent nation—the
very centre of endless processes of our country's industry and prosperity. Like the heart in the human body, which sends its throbbing pulsations
through all the arteries and veins, bearing life, nour-
ishment and vigor, so has it, through all our civil,
political, commercial, financial and productive systems, united and assimilated increasing millions in
one vast giant confederacy, which has stretched its
vigorous growth across the continent, nearly from
the frozen region of the north, to the torrid equa-
torial climes. Its power and glory have astonished
the world, as by the blessings of Divine Providence
it has turned the desert into an Eden, and made
the wilderness to blossom as the rose. Like the
Orient sun, it has poured forth its radiant beams,
waxing in its strength, as its splendor advanced,
from hemisphere to hemisphere, and illumined the
globe. While wretchedness, tyranny and crime set-
tled in deep midnight gloom on other lands, and
wars and desolation filled their inhabitants with
consternation and horror, here all was prosperity
and happiness, grandeur and glory, under its vital-
izing power. Like the gravitating force which
gives stability to the earth, it has been the *primum
mobile* of our Union, which nothing but violence,
like earthquake throes, could rend. The volcanic
fires of mad, impetuous passion alone, confined and
struggling beneath our foundations, and not external
violence, are the only source of danger to the stability and perpetuity of that constitution, which, for

nearly three-quarters of a century, has harmonized and united this great confederacy.

But now alarm exists extensively, lest dangers from this source are close upon us. Quivering shocks, spasmodic tremblings, and heaving undulations, have sent the thrill of terror into myriads of palpitating hearts. The governing authorities, the veteran statesmen, the wise and sober counselors, and devoted patriots, are not without solicitude and fears. Should passion reign, and the great God of nations, who has hitherto protected and preserved us, withdraw His guardianship, our securities are gone. If once "He arises to shake terribly the earth," our lofty, proud and stable edifice must topple to the ground. Who can estimate the ruin that a few moments of such earthquake shocks, the revolutionary violence of wild, careering fires of passion, may produce? Time may indeed repair them; but at what an immense expenditure of life, and property, and labor! The rending of the bonds that hold these States in union, the secession and separation of one or more, by open, violent rejection and defiance of constitutional compacts, must prove the first throes of disastrous revolutions, in long succession, beyond all power of human sagacity to foresee, or human wisdom and might to arrest and counteract. Thus did they in the history of the separation of the tribes of Israel. Our prosperity, our safety, our hope as a nation, depend upon a wisdom and a power that can hush the hurtling tempest, and quench the smouldering, struggling fires, or open some volcanic vent, like the safety valve, and bid them exhaust themselves at their leisure. God alone can give the wisdom to do this. He, only, is competent to apply the hand that shall save. The rule of His providence, illustrated and established in the history of other nations, and as mighty as our own, is applicable to us in present circumstances. "At what instant I speak concerning a nation, and concerning a kingdom; to pluck up and to pull down, and to destroy it; if that nation against whom I have pronounced, turn from their evil, I will repent of the evil that I thought to do unto it." Repentance and reformation, sustaining an appeal to Him, will as truly save our country now, as it ever did Nineveh, or Israel, or Judah, or our sires of revolutionary piety and patriotism.

Third. But here a third question is pertinent: How are such repentance and reformation to be secured? It will be, as it often has been, asked, how are we, as a people, to turn from the evil which has caused God in His providence to pronounce against us? One party says, abolish slavery; another says, violate no longer constitutional compacts. Criminations and recriminations have thence arisen. Taunts, jeers, reproaches, daring and provoking challenges, on the one hand, exasperate and madden. Unfounded allegations and passionate phrenzy, excited by misapprehension, misrepresentation, suspicions, and fallacious reasonings, on the other hand, are thrown back with intense violence. Interests are found in conflict. Reason is blinded by passion. The complications and surroundings of the policies of antagonistic parties admit not of prompt, easy, categorical adjustment. Morally and religiously, judgment, conscience, and feeling, among great masses of our population, are found at variance.

The question of slavery has already divided North and South, as really in a moral, and ecclesiastical, and social point of view, as were the tribes of Israel separated in the days of Rehoboam, and Jeroboam. And Jerusalem and Samaria were not more effectually made the seat and centres of discordant and uncongenial, moral and commercial systems, than the agitation of this subject seems to have prepared the way for Charleston and New York, or Boston to become the focus, of rival opposing and antagonistic systems of religions, as well as of political and commercial influence. The breach in the confederacy of the twelve tribes of the Jewish nation—which confederacy, to some extent, formed the model, and suggested many of the principles incorporated in our own—became irremediable, from the moment that the religious and social feelings were alienated, and gathered around Mount Gerizim and Mount Moriah, as the seats and centres of rival and opposing systems of spiritual influence. In such a state of things, amid the ruins of divided churches, the question becomes agitating and alarming; is it posible, can any thing be done to prevent repellent and abhorrent feelings, sustained by rival and opposing fanaticisms, from producing lasting and incurable alienations and disunions? Here, here precisely, is where we feel that the greatest danger lies. The South have their religious views and feelings, accordant with the teachings of their pulpits, and the trainings of education, on the subject of slavery. The North have theirs. Neither seem prepared, soberly and considerately to apply the spirit of Christ and the teachings of the Scriptures, in the exercise of forbearance and brotherly regards, for the solution of the various entangling and intricate questions of sin and duty connected with it.

The spirit of repentance and reformation in both is indispensable, for the exercise of sound judgment and a good conscience in the premises, and for securing the help and favor of Divine Providence. But our case is by no means desperate. There are some things which can be done, and the religious and christian portion of the country must initiate them.

Let it be made known and fully understood, that the compromises of the constitution shall be faithfully kept and honestly carried out, so that an example be given, of practical respect for the sacredness of social compacts, and of an abiding sense of moral obligation. Let party spirit and sectional strifes give place to patriotic love of country. Let angry denunciations, and a bitter spirit of mutual crimination and animosity, be supplanted by the friendly feeling of one common citizenship, and the regards of fraternal good will and affection. Let a reckless partisan and venal press be rebuked, and a public sentiment be formed, founded on truth, and right, and loyal attachment to the Union of these States. Let the patriotic devotion, which inspired our sires with invincible attachment to one common cause and country, inspire their sons, and make us true to the constitution and government they founded. Let there be a return to the principles and policy which characterized the administration of Washington. Let the government be administered, not for private emolument, or party victors, or sectional interests and ambitions, or theoretical purposes, or schemes of political aggrandizement, or territorial acquisitions and conquests; but for the public good. Let moneyed aristocracies, and chartered monopolies, and secret conspiracies of trade, and transported nationalities, and privileged and corrupt corporations, bow before the majesty of a virtuous people, bent on the maintenance of equal rights, and the diffusion, as far as practicable, of the greatest amount of equality in social condition, in wealth, and in education. Let men of integrity, and worthy of trust, be elevated to office, and none be called to discharge the functions of authority, who are ignorant, incapable, and reckless of social and moral obligation. Let the judge, or legislator, or public functionary, known to receive a bribe, or make his official duty truckle to his selfish and pecuniary interest, be punishable for criminal offense, and forever ineligible to any office. Let the laws be faithfully executed by the officers appointed for that purpose. And let penalties, specifically provided for by law, be imposed on every officer, sworn to perform the duties of his office, who neglects, fails, or refuses to discharge the same, or to render the service required by the law for its enforcement.

The want of concurrent fidelity on the part of magistrates and officers, in the enforcement of law, will be sure to frustrate any and every attempt at general repentance and reformation. The spirit of lawlessness abroad in the land—which tramples compacts under feet, and defies the execution of laws for good order and the general good—is the legitimate result of examples, set by governmental authorities, from the highest to the lowest, who have betrayed and abused the trust reposed in them as public functionaries and guardians of the general weal. When magistrates and public officers are profane swearers, Sabbath breakers, drunkards, liars, scoffers at religion, covetous, oppressors, and violators of law themselves, the greatest obstacles are thrown in the way of public repentance and reformation. The guilt of perjury is thus superadded to all other miscarriages and personal sins. Wrath from God accumulates rapidly against a people that will consent to such a state of things.

Ministers of religion, and people at large, must aim at, and carry on a work of repentance and reformation, where such things exist, if they would turn away the judgments of God, impending over a guilty land. No work of repentance or reformation ever was carried on among a people, where the laws against flagitious immoralities were not enforced, and men entrusted with power did not evince that it was their determination to have offenders punished. Joshua, David, Hezekiah, and others, accomplished wonders, by their zealous fidelity in the discharge of their official trusts and obligations. And true, reliable, and faithful rulers yet can accomplish marvelous results. Let but the Sunday laws, and the prohibitory liquor laws, and others against vice and immorality, be faithfully executed, and we shall quickly see a work of repentance and reformation prevail to turn away impending judgments from the land.

A very large amount of our national guilt is to be traced to the Sabbath desecration and intemperance, that have disgraced our halls of legislation, from the Common Councils of our cities, up to the State Legislatures, and the Congress of the United States. No wonder if God, in His providence, should turn His hand against us, to smite us with the rod of His displeasure, and let the demons of discord and confusion loose among us, if we neglect the obligations of morality and good faith. He does not ordinarily bring wasting and desolating judgments on a people or nation, without having given previous warning of their approach; and never without good reason for it. For 120 years, He admonished the world for its wickedness, before He overthrew it with a flood. Sodom and Gomorrha perished not, till after they had rejected the counsel and admonition of Lot, and utterly corrupted themselves. Jerusalem and Judah, Samaria and Israel, Egypt and Nineveh, and Tyre, and Babylon, and Greece, and all the great nations of antiquity, which have perished, had their warnings and seasons of repentance and reformation, that postponed for a season the crisis of their ruin. That came not, till they became regardless of warning, and hardened themselves in their wickedness.

The nations of modern Europe have had their days of warning; and judgment has delayed, as they have repented and turned from their wickedness. We are yet a young nation. Our crimes have not yet filled up the cup of our iniquity. God has lavished favors on us. No nation under heaven has shared so largely of His bounties as we have done. He has been loath to give us up. The corner stone of our great edifice was laid in faith, and prayer ascending from the hearts of many devout patriots and saints of God. He has yet much people in this land. The gospel here is yet cherished, and spreads its hallowing influence among us. Schools, colleges, institutions of learning, charity, and piety, rear their attractive towers. Churches of the living God flourish, and multiply still among us. Again and again has He poured out His Spirit upon us; and the people having extensively repented and turned from their wickedness, He has turned His wrath from us. God seems loath to abandon us. He loves us for the fathers' sake; and He is saying: "How shall I give thee up, Ephraim? How shall I deliver thee, Israel? How shall I make thee as Admah? How shall I set thee as Zeboim? My heart is turned within me: my repentings are kindled together."

Much as there is ground to fear, there is still more for hope. We have His pledge, that if we repent of the evils we have done, He will repent of the evil He thought to do unto us. If He has sent a panic, originating in political causes, to alarm and excite dismay, He has done it, under circumstances when its results may be most easily obviated. In the midst of plenty, in the midst of rejoicings, the alarm is sounded that we be not surfeited with excess. And can we not discern obstacles, marked and peculiar, thrown by His providence in the way of impetuous passion, and of the wild and frantic strife for which the bugle blasts have here and there been already blown? The contrast of condition, in fiscal matters, between the North and South, has thrown power into the hands of those called to forbearance and prudence, and taken it from those whose voice is lifted up for severance and disunion. Foreign and domestic exchanges are greatly in favor of the former. The materiel of prosperity is profusely laid to their hands. A wholesome check is given to reckless banking. Never could there have been circumstances less propitious to division, and less open and public pretext for violence. Political parties broken into fragments! The dominant majority in the choice of their chief magistrate at a fearful dead lock, as to power to do harm should they be so disposed! Division of counsel and confusion of purpose among the separatists! Our great national Congress on the eve of assembling! The Federal Executive authorities, calm, firm, and determined to exert their power wisely, energetically, and without unnecessary irritation and exasperation! The chief magistrate elect, uncommitted to violent measures; untrammeled by party discipline; untarnished by reproach even from his foes; unshaken in the confidence of his friends; undisturbed by the noise of surrounding excitement; unmoved in the majesty of dignified composure and silence; and quietly waiting the summons of Providence, to assume and discharge the solemn and heavy responsibilities to be devolved upon him! Can we not see in all this, the ordering of a propitious providence? God, as it were, is waiting for this great nation to turn from its evil, and thus give Him occasion for prolonging His care, and turning away the evil He had seen that we were bringing on ourselves!

Should we not, then, in our grateful offerings this day, for the lavish bounties He has scattered round us, deeply ponder the rule of His providence, applicable to our present circumstances as a nation? And, while repenting of the evils we have done and consented to, should we not hopefully lift our imploring and believing cry,—"Spare, Lord, our guilty land; give not thy heritage to reproach; suffer not the tie that binds us as one to be rent asunder! But, as thou hast been our fathers' God; and led them through the wilderness; and established them in this good land; be thou also the God of their children; and to generations yet unborn, transmit, unbroken, unharmed, and enhanced, the privileges, liberty and union of these confederate States."

Oh, God! look down upon the land which Thou hast loved so well,
And grant that in unbroken truth her children still may dwell;
Nor, while the grass grows on the hill, and streams flow through the vale,
May they forget their father's, or in their covenant fail!
God keep the fairest, noblest land that lies beneath the sun:
"Our country, our whole country, and our country ever ONE."

OUR NATIONAL SINS TO BE REPENTED OF,

AND THE

Grounds of Hope for the Preservation

OF OUR

FEDERAL CONSTITUTION AND UNION.

A DISCOURSE

DELIVERED

FRIDAY, JANUARY 4, 1861,

ON THE

DAY OF FASTING, HUMILIATION AND PRAYER

APPOINTED BY THE PRESIDENT OF THE UNITED STATES.

BY GEORGE DUFFIELD,
PASTOR OF THE FIRST PRESBYTERIAN CONGREGATION OF DETROIT.

DETROIT:
FREE PRESS MAMMOTH BOOK AND JOB PRINTING HOUSE.
1861.

A DISCOURSE.

1. **PSALM 78: 37, 39.** Their heart was not right with Him, neither were they steadfast in His covenant. But He being full of compassion, forgave their iniquity and destroyed them not; yea, many a time turned He His anger away, and did not stir up all His wrath; for He remembered that they were but flesh; a wind that passeth away and cometh not again.

2. **PSALM 79: 8, 9.** O remember not against us former iniquities: let Thy tender mercies speedily prevent us; for we are brought very low. Help us, O God of our salvation, for the glory of Thy name; and deliver us and purge away our sins, for Thy names' sake.

BUT five weeks have passed, since we assembled in this place, to render our thanks to Almighty God, for His great goodness to us as a nation. A dark cloud then had risen above our horizon, portentous, to some, of a coming storm. But the mass of politicians and people had either not noticed, or did not regard it, then, as at all ominous of evil. We took occasion to press the admonition, as intimated by the divine providence, to rejoice with fear and trembling, and to mingle repentings and humblings of heart before God for our sins, with our thanksgivings.

To-day we assemble, in accordance with the proclamation of the President of the United States, to implore the mercy and forgiveness of God, in the midst of discord, perplexity and perils. "Hope," says he, "seems to have deserted the minds of men. All classes are in a state of confusion and dismay, and the wisest counsels of our best and purest men are wholly disregarded. In this, the hour of our calamity and peril, to whom shall we resort for relief, but to the God of our fathers? His omnipotent arm only, can save us from the awful effects of our own crimes and follies, our ingratitude and guilt towards our Heavenly Father." The trumpet of alarm has been blown from the very citadel. In bewilderment and trepidation, the head of the army, cabinet, civil government, and this once flourishing confederacy, invokes the nation to repentance and confession of individual and national sins; "to acknowledge God's justice in their punishment; to implore Him to remove from our hearts the false pride that might prompt to persevere in wrong; to restore the good will and friendship of former days between the people of our several States; to save us from the horrors of civil war and "blood-guiltiness;" to "desert us not in this hour of extreme peril, but to remember us as He did our fathers, in the darkest days of the revolution, and preserve our Constitution and our Union, the works of their hands, for ages yet to come."

These are all matters legitimate and appropriate to the present exigencies. Whatever different persons may think of the spirit, and motives, and policy of the President, it ill becomes any one, especially members, elders, and ministers of the church of Christ to set an example of party spirit, pride of opinion, disrespect for the highest governmental authority, and thus sanction the lawlessness, contempt of rule, and atheistic idea of liberty prevalent, by refusing to unite in an humble appeal to God for our common country, at the request of the chief magistracy. This is virtually to aid and abet the scoffs and sneers of the infidel partisan, "the wicked," who, as the psalmist says, "through the pride of his countenance will not seek after God," "whose judgments are far above out of his sight; who puffeth at his enemies, and saith in his heart, there is no danger, we shall not be moved, we shall never see adversity." * Even should there be bewilderment, misapprehension, neglect of duty, or worse— so that there might be reason to fear the betrayal of trust, or the manifestation of imbecility on the part of those to whose courage, and wisdom, and counsels, the management of the great affairs of State is confided—the greater is the reason, the louder is the call of providence, to make an appeal to the God of our fathers, and enroll our names under His banner, when He demands "Who is on the Lord's side?" "Who will rise up for Me against the evil doer? or who will stand up for me against the workers of iniquity?" †

"Shall a trumpet be blown in the city, and the people not be afraid? Shall there be evil in a city and the Lord hath not done it?" ‡ Whatever we may think about the political and partisan causes, that have led to the present trouble and tumults

---

* Psalm 10 : 4, 6.　　† Psalm 94 : 16.　　‡ Amos 3 : 6.

among the people of this land; however foolishly or wisely and reproachfully, men may talk and reason about the nature and sources of the peril and perplexity of the country, the Lord's hand is in it. "The Lord God of hosts," the prophet says, "is He that toucheth the land, and it shall melt, and all that dwell therein shall mourn." * If He had not seen sin in us, and we had not, in some way, as a people sorely displeased Him, He had not smitten us, and brought upon us the things we fear. It is His righteous providence that has commanded and raised the stormy wind, which lifteth up the waves that toss the great ship of State like a foundering bark upon the billows, and cause our rulers to reel to and fro, to stagger like a drunken man, and be at their wits' end.

It is well that there is a God to whom we may pray. As many a bewildered crew upon the stormy deep, when their creaking, shattered vessel has mounted up to the heavens, and gone down again to the depths, and their soul melted because of trouble, have cried unto the Lord, and He brought them out of their distress, and made the storm a calm, so that the waves thereof were still; so has He done for us as a people—and so can He again do, and will—what all human wisdom and valor cannot accomplish, if we call upon Him with penitent and believing hearts, in this day of our calamity.

The passages of Scripture we have selected and

---

* Amos 9 : 5.

read, as a guide and foundation for our reflections, are full of encouragement, and unfold to us abundant sources of hope. The one shows what God, replete with mercy and compassion, was willing to do, and often had done, for a people whose sins and iniquities had forfeited all just claim upon Him. The other is the prayer we may be emboldened to offer, if with penitent and believing hearts we seek forgiveness, purification, and the interposition of divine aid. The motives and argument of such prayer are to be derived from His own merciful nature, the abounding of His compassions in Jesus Christ, who is the glorious name of God—the embodiment and manifestation of His own infinite and adorable excellence—the brightness of the Father's Glory, the express image of His person, the only hope and standing plea for mercy, at all available and efficacious, for a guilty sinner or a guilty people.

That we may, intelligently and in faith, present our supplications to God this day, on our country's behalf, we propose to inquire:

I. What are the sins for which God is contending with us as a nation?

II. On what grounds we may venture to pray for the preservation of the Constitution and the Union of our national confederacy?

Every form and variety of sin and crime among a people does not deserve to be called national, however it may swell the amount of popular guilt. National sins are those, and those only, which, by reason of their commonness, frequency, popularity, and the state, grade, and condition of those who commit

them, are allowed to pass, either without the pro-
hibition of law, or without punishment by the enforcement of law. Government is ordained of God
for the protection of society against evil, and for
the promotion of the public good. The moral law,
or law of the ten commandments, is God's legislation against crime, for the individual and general
good. It lies at the foundation, and should ever be
magnified as the basis, of all civil, political, and
criminal statutes. Whatever tends to subvert the
authority of the moral law, in any of its great
organic provisions, and conflicts, or is inconsistent
with its spirit and precepts, is, and ever must be,
injurious to the peace, purity, and safety of individual citizens, and to the public good.

What are the gross sins, against which God has
denounced national judgments, and which, when un-
restrained and unpunished by the civil magistracy,
He, in His providence, will visit with the rod of
His chastisement, the sacred Scriptures have clearly
declared, and abundantly illustrated in various his-
torical precedents therein recorded. Ordinarily, He
does not interfere by any temporal visitations of
His punitive providence, to correct the crimes
of men, where the magistrates or governmental
authorities are attentive and faithful to their obligations in this respect. For such interposition is
thereby rendered unnecessary. But, where they neglect their duties, and the people love, or consent, to
have it so, and will elevate to, and sustain in office,
corrupt men, so that the laws against the vices of
society become a dead letter, and crimes prevail on

every hand, there is nothing left for the general welfare and safety, but for God to interfere with His retributive judgments. Accordingly, He has said, "when the land sinneth against Me by trespassing grievously, then will I stretch out my hand." *

The most superficial observer cannot fail to discover, in this country, the prevalence of various forms of vice, which have been tolerated and practiced so extensively in society, that judgments from the hand of God have fallen upon us, frequently and extensively. Often have they been so marked, that they could not well be mistaken. Such are the intemperance in all classes,—the utter disrespect of truth—the prevalent falsehood and frauds in business, social intercourse, and the press,—the want of good faith and fidelity in the trusts and relations of life—the desecration of the Sabbath—the contempt of compacts and oaths and obligations of office—profanity—licentiousness—lawlessness—oppression—polygamy among the Mormons—adultery, sanctioned by divorce laws—avaricious extortion—and swindling operations of speculators, bankers and corporations almost without end, which almost every where in our land corrupt society. Of these, and such like, the legislation and government of our several States have immediate and principal cognizance. However widely diffused are such, and kindred forms of vice and immorality, which, by reason of general extent may be, or become, national, all our

---

* Ezekiel 14: 13.

different States are not equally involved in the growing corruption and consequent condemnation.

In estimating our national crimes, reference must be had to the peculiar features and functions of our Federal government.

The want of any recognition of God, in the constitution of the United States, and even in the form of the Presidential oath of office which it prescribes, taken in connection with its declaration of absolute, unqualified sovereignty of the people, as the source of its authority, and the supreme law of the land, affords apparent and formal ground for this charge. The christian forms of oath, as sometimes, and commonly in the States, administered under it to different United States' officers, and the opinions and ruling of some of our State Judges, may, in practice have somewhat mitigated this charge: but, unquestionably, there is—in that non-recognition of Almighty God, and of Jesus Christ, the Lord of Lords and King of Kings, by whom princes decree justice, and of the divine authority of the sacred Scriptures—sufficient reason to awake the fears, as it has ever done, of many virtuous, sober-minded, religious citizens, that its unqualified and virtually atheistic claim of popular sovereignty, irrespective of the law, the word, and the providence of God our Saviour, may have subjected us, as a nation, so far to His displeasure, as, to have forfeited for us the perpetuity of the Federal government, it established as the bond of union, and to secure, eventually, a demonstration from Him, of the danger and licentious excesses of a liberty—and the weakness, folly, and falsehood of any asserted right or ability for self-government—independent of Jehovah, and unrestricted by His supreme, universal, immutable law, and the counsels of His holy Scriptures.

It has been thought also, and much more frequently, extensively, and confidently affirmed, that the slavery practiced in this land forms THE great national sin. On this account, more than any other, it has been, and is, as confidently believed and proclaimed, that mainly, if not exclusively, the Lord is dealing with us in His providence, and threatening to pull down upon our heads the fair and noble structure of this confederacy. The evils and the crimes, however, either incident to or involved in the system of southern slavery—which makes human persons property equally with chattels and cattle, and thus degrades human beings originally created in the image of God,—do not, as we think, implicate directly, either the Constitution of the United States, or the compact under it, or all of the States, much less the citizens, generally, of our confederacy. Were this the fact, we could have no faith or hope in the efficacy of prayer to God to preserve and perpetuate our Union. For we can cherish no hope of permanent security and prosperity for any people or nation whatever, if its constitution, or legislation under it, should be in direct and flagrant violation of any of the great fundamental provisions of the law of God, the moral law, or law of the ten commandments, especially as expounded in the Scriptures by our Lord and Savior Jesus Christ.

Whether slavery, as it exists in our country, is in violation of that law of God, which is the law of love, holy, and just, and good, and true, requiring us to do to others as we would have them do to us, is a question of deep and vital moment. The moral bearing and aspect of this question, we have ever thought, should have been examined and discussed, testified and proclaimed, in the spirit of love and forbearance. The church in this matter should have been the witness of Christ. From the moment it became entangled with party political strifes, and the slavery question and discussions began to assume a sectional consequence, through the collisions of interest, commerce, politics, and struggles for office and authority, we feared, and averred, that the results would prove disastrous.

The attributes of slavery in the South, are to be mainly traced, in the statutary codes, the social regulations, practices, and habits, with their legitimate fruits, in the different States, where, by local laws it is defined, characterized, protected and maintained, both as a species of chattel property and a domestic institution, forming an element, or entering into the very structure, of the civil State, but not of general national society. The Federal constitution, while it recognizes a right to service from one human person to another, degrades not our common humanity by making men property like beasts of burden.

The original patriarchal idea of servitude, recognized in the Bible history of Abraham, although sophistically referred to by the advocates of American slavery as its "sanction," went no further. Such, also, was the slavery originally, to a great extent, if not generally, in our own country, anterior to the adoption of the Federal constitution. All of the colonies had more or less of it in them before the American Revolution. In all but Massachusetts it still existed at the adoption of the Federal constitution. Whatever, and however, great were the evils and sins to which slavery led, the slaveholder was not regarded as a sinner above all others; nor slavery as criminal under all circumstances, and the very worst of crimes. The Northern and some of the Middle States repented of it— modified as it then was in them, in accordance with the letter of the constitution, and its spirit,—and put it away, by a wise and salutary system of gradual emancipation, believing, that what God denounced by Noah as a curse upon Canaan, neither was, nor ever could be, meant by Him to be understood and practiced as a blessing, and desirable in the social state.

Nevertheless, commercial interests and relations, various social ties of marriage, kindred, trade, bequest, and enterprises of business, involve, no doubt, a considerable portion of the citizens of our free States, indirectly and incidentally, as well as directly in the guilt and evils of this thing, and thence, create a sympathy and sensitiveness touching it, which often, and naturally, expresses itself in the conflicts and platforms of party politics. But, by no public act of organic law or of their governments, can it be said, that the free States have made themselves partakers of the sins of slavery, appropriate and peculiar to the degrading of human beings or persons, by making and regarding them as chattel property.

Some, indeed, have contended that they did so, by the adoption, first, of the Federal constitution, and, subsequently, of the Missouri compromise, in 1820, and especially by the legislation of Congress, pursuant to the constitutional compact, requiring fidelity in carrying out its provisions, relative to the rendition of fugitives. A party, in a few of the free States, especially Massachusetts and Pennsylvania—whose leaders have been characterized by what we regard the most arrant infidelity, and repudiation of the plenary and miraculous inspiration and divine authority of the sacred scriptures, zealous, mistaken fanatics—under erroneous pleas of philanthropy, have, while blaspheming the word of God, denounced the Federal Constitution and Union as fraught with guilt, sufficient to provoke the judgments of heaven. Their language and abuse of Washington and the constitution, it is not fitting here to quote; but they have thought they were doing service to both God and man, especially the slave, to rend and destroy our Union. We have never been able to see that their construction of the constitution is just, or capable of being sustained; either by the legitimate meaning of the language, or by the debates and history of the convention that formed it, and of the legislatures that adopted it. The Missouri compromise—which indeed changed the policy of the Federal administration and the dominant party, and which we deplored at the time as mischievous, however it may have been a great mistake—was nevertheless conceived and formed in 1820, for the maintenance of treaty-faith, pledged as it was thought, in the purchase of Louisiana.

Immediate and *unqualified* emancipation began in 1833–4, to be proclaimed and demanded by certain moral and political extremists, as the only proof of repentance, and the only salvation of the country. And because the Constitution of the United States neither possesses, nor could be made by amendment to possess, power to accomplish this, whatever might increase the friction and hasten the dissolution of the Union, found ready and cordial entertainment and sympathy.

Many of the ministry, and members of different evangelical churches, were zealously affected with the thought of immediate emancipation as alike the duty and safety of our country. The relation of master and slave, slavery *per se*, without any reserve or qualification whatever, was pronounced a God-provoking sin, the greatest men can commit, and all involved in that relationship denounced as guilty of man-stealing, robbery, murder, and whatever other crimes are incident to the system as spread out in the statutes, sustained by law, and, in flagrant cases, carried into practice, in all, or any of the southern States! This rampant zeal—sustained, as we have ever thought, by fallacious logic—agitated and rent churches, united ecclesiastically, and previously walking in harmonious christian fellowship. It engendered alienations, strifes and divisions between Congregationalists and Presbyterians; repudiated the plan of union upon which they had, for more than the third of a century, happily co-operated; separated them completely as distinct and rival denominations; drove the ploughshare of division between the northern and southern churches; and carried the war of angry debate and irreconcilable antagonisms, into the different great national associations for missionary and tract operations.

The judgment of a large portion of the ministry and churches, in the southern States, and also in the northern, could not see and admit, either the obligation, the benevolence, the practicability, or the safety of immediate emancipation, as then and thus urged. The consciences of multitudes who sustained the relation of master to slave, did not, or could not be made to feel, that the simple relationship of master to slave, or slavery under all circumstances, was sinful; and especially, when they knew, that there were obligations of guardianship, dictates of humanity, and claims of enlightened charity, which not only forbade immediate and unqualified emancipation, but required the continuance of that relation and sometimes its formation. From the denunciations of those—who neither saw nor would admit such obligations, but who held them up to scorn and infamy, and sought *to excommunicate them by declarative resolutions* from the church of God, as unworthy a place in it—they turned away, and said, "how can two walk together unless they be agreed!" preferring secession and separation to strife and obloquy.

In their attempts to interpret the report of their own consciences, which acquitted them from the false, unqualified charges of guilt, made against them by their northern brethren, they found themselves in circumstances where the temptation became natural and powerful, to justify slavery as a system, as well as to excuse all its developments, and exonerate themselves from the criminality personally and promiscuously charged upon them. Inasmuch as the Bible,—which gives an account of God's civil legislation concerning slavery, and the counsels and precepts of divine wisdom in relation to the moral duties and obligations growing out of the relation of christians to it, and to the governments that tolerated or enacted it,—has thus distinctly recognized the existence of that relation, and enjoined reciprocal duties on masters and servants, the judgment and conscience of southern ministers and churches began to claim, what none of a former generation had ever thought of doing, that God, by such legislation, had SANCTIONED it, and made it as truly a DIVINE ORDINANCE as He had government itself; and that, indeed, it was but a species of government, provided and ordained by His wisdom and benevolence for the benefit of the domestic and social state. Rev. Mr. H. J. Van Dyke, of Brooklyn, and Dr. Palmer, of New Orleans, have volunteered their casuistry in this matter, as a writer in Mississippi, years ago, had done, in opposition to the ultra views of immediate emancipation that had been inculcated and propagated in the North. It is proof to us of the blinding influence, which sympathy with party

2a

politics, and polemic casuistry, can exert upon the mind and conscience. These excellent brethren seem not for one moment to have adverted to what is undeniably true, that God, when legislating as the civil head of Israel,—just as human governments ever find it necessary for them to do,—enacted laws in view of evils nascent or innate in corrupt society, for the purpose of restricting, restraining, and ultimately curing them; and that such legislation is far, very far, from implying His *allowance* or *approval*, much less His *sanction* of them. To claim that slavery is a divine ordinance, because God has legislated concerning it, indicates, either an inability or unwillingness, through prejudice or passion, to distinguish between enduring a present evil, in a given state of society for the prevention of greater, and sanctioning such evil in every condition of society. Never was there a greater nonsequitur, more palpable and offensive sophistry, than that into which these writers have been betrayed.

Such casuistry has been one of the melancholy results of the alienations and separations produced in the churches by the political agitation of this subject. Shut out and cut off from the sympathy of the churches and the christian community, generally, of the North, the southern churches and christians, very naturally, received and relished the sympathy of unbelieving men and political partisans, who, from mistaken considerations of State and national policy, were seeking to protect and propagate and perpetuate the slavery, in connection with which they had been born and nursed, *educated* and *trained.* Nor have the ministry and churches at the North been wholly exempt from a similar and hurtful influence upon their judgment and consciences, by sympathy with political partisanships, inducing a rancorous spirit of denunciation often mistaken for, and claimed to be, a superior piety.

The essential and irreconcileable antagonism between free labor and slave labor can never be cured, permanently and completely, by any system of human legislation that attempts to harmonize them. Light and darkness are not more at variance, radically and immutably, than are liberty and bondage. The conflict between them has well been pronounced, by one of our eminent statesmen, "irrepressible." Compacts and legislation may ease its violence; and, if wise and just, lead to the gradual salutary disappearance of the one before the other. But the experiments of past ages and nations from the first, have proved, in the recorded history of mankind, that freedom and slavery cannot dwell permanently, harmoniously, safely, and prosperously, together.

God's legislation on the subject, found in the book of Leviticus, so far from being a sanction of slavery, was actually a wise and wonderful system of gradual, but certain and inevitable emancipation. The history of the Jewish nation proved and illustrated it.

The patriarchal slavery, claimed to have been sanctioned by the example of Abraham, was not hereditary. There is no proof that it descended to Isaac or Ishmael. Certainly none that it was

transmitted to Jacob and Esau, in the third generation.

God's ethical precepts on the subject in the New
Testament, on which Mr. Van Dyke and others
have founded their erring deductions, were explicitly
designed, as the context shows, not to *sanction* the
political code and usages of the Roman Empire; but
to bring out and exhibit, in the clearest and strongest
possible light, the moral power of that christian benevolence, which makes the master and the slave
alike feel that they are brethren of one family, and
which is a much more potent force, to remedy and
overcome the evils and existence of slavery, than
any mere political expedients, or system of civil
legislation, that human wisdom without it can ever
devise.

The extremists' views, on both sides of this question, and in both sections of our country, which have,
for the last twenty-six years, been pressed in various
political and ecclesiastical contests, have resulted in
deep, permanent, and, we fear, fatal estrangements.
The doctrines of immediate emancipation, and of the
sin of slavery *per se*, as taught by ultra abolitionists,
have irritated the South far more than personal liberty
bills, or the election of a republican candidate for
the President. The pro-slavery teachings and violence of southern preachers and politicians, have, in
their turn, exasperated the North. The thrift and
prosperity of the North, their progress in wealth,
population, and improvement, whatever may have
been the policy of the Federal government, —
forcing, at one time into commerce, another manu-

factures, and at another free trade—have proved so illustrative and demonstrative of the value and efficiency of free labor, as to have increasingly excited the envy, jealousy, and rivalry of the South, whose exhausted farms, dilapidated domiciles, disordered finances, mortgaged property, depreciated lands, and other evidences of decay, made them look, with an angry and suspicious eye, upon the commerce, manufactures, enterprise, capital, resources, and enhanced prosperity of the free States. Socially, politically, religiously, there have been developed, and are, antagonisms, which have already rent the most solemn compacts, and destroyed the most sacred sympathies. How they are to be reconciled, if possible, is the great problem of the day, which leaves all our sages and statesmen utterly at fault. Well has the President, in his proclamation for a fast, invited one and all, both North and South, to implore God to remove "the false pride of heart which impels, for consistency's sake, to persevere in wrong." It is God only who can do it.

Concession, without the sacrifice of moral principle, and in the spirit of forbearance and forgiveness, may, and we would fain hope, by God's blessing, will do it. Crimination and recrimination, charges of provocation and blame primarily and mainly, by either party, will never accomplish it. Civil war and bloodshed will render it forever impossible. Here, in this very pride of opinion, we think, lies much of the guilt, the peril and perplexity connected with the question of slavery in our Federal relations. If the North will consent that the South adjust for themselves the evils of their own social state, and, ceasing to traduce, denounce, and vituperate, will extend to them the good will and charities of christian brotherhood; and *if* the South will not insist upon extending the acknowledged evils of their own social state, by demanding their admission and approbation in new States and Territories, there to spread and prolong this cancer in the body politic, there may be hope. But *if* the North can only be reconciled, on the ground of anti-slavery propagandism within the southern States, or the South, upon the ground of the extension of slavery by right of their construction of the constitution; and *if* the constitution must be changed to meet the views of either, then is our unity forever at an end. The antagonisms of party should never regulate the administration of our government. It should be conducted on higher principles. If the pride of opinion and the oppositions of party, cannot be overcome, by the spirit of patriotism and devotion to the public good, there can be no safe and peaceful deliverance for us from our present perplexities. The gaping fissures must increase. The separation must become fragmentary; and dissolution follow, without hope or possibility of ever again crystallizing or aggregating, in the same or any other happy consolidated Union, similar to that, which, for more than half a century, has made us, as a nation, the wonder and glory of the world.

Our social, political, moral and religious strength as a nation hitherto, has been in our union. The one tie, that binds all together, once severed and acknowledged to be so, divides not, by a wide and yawning chasm. As in the human body, the disintegrating process of dissolution supervenes, the moment that the vital forces, through their constitutional channels, cease to operate; so will and must it be in the national. Discordant interests, rival factions, predatory incursions, servile insurrections, despotic oppressions, rapacious robberies, contending ambitions, selfish demagogism, phrenzied excitements, hostile religions, civil wars degenerating into contests of aspiring military chieftains, and intriguing schemes of corrupt monopolies and men of wealth, will not fail to repeat, in more aggravated and distressing story, the revolutions and disasters of disordered, wretched, ruined Mexico. May the God of heaven mercifully interpose to prevent it!

We fear, however, that the complications and exacerbation of this great moral, social and political evil of slavery, around which the eyes and hearts, the hopes and fears, the anxieties and lamentations of the nation this day cluster, may be traced to a guilt, even more strictly national than it, and which, we have judged and felt for nearly the third of a century, is the great public national crime God is now punishing, by the present agitation, excitement and alarm, as He has been in years past, by various processes of demoralization. The slavery trouble has been the entering wedge and battle axe, that quickly followed, with its strokes of wrath, after the offense of which we shall now speak.

By treaty both with Georgia, and with the

Indians in the territory, which she ceded to the United States, the Cherokee Indians were put under the fostering care of the Federal government. Their lands, eight million acres of which they refused to sell, were recognized as their own, and reserved to them, by solemn treaty. Their absolute title to them was admitted to be beyond the power of the States or of Congress, and to be alienated only, by treaties honorably and fairly made, and with full assent of their own. Missionaries were established among them, under the direction and support of the American Board of Commissioners of Foreign Missions, and of other missionary associations of different religious denominations. By express stipulations, on the part of the United States Government, a limited territory, protection, and inviolate territorial limits, were guaranteed to the Cherokee nation of Indians. They had attained to civilization, and established among themselves the trades, arts, and religion, upon the lands of their ancestors. Having, by the advice of the President of the United States, organized a government of their own, consisting of legislative, judiciary, and executive departments, administered on republican principles, they had risen in character, condition, and prospects; and were bound to us as brothers, by the ties of that christianity, which, in common with us, they had professed. But it was discovered that their lands contained gold.

Georgia claimed, that according to her construction of the treaty with the United States government, by which she ceded her territory, the Federal government had failed to fulfill its provisions of that treaty; although

Washington, Jefferson, Jackson, and Calhoun, had been the foster-fathers of the citizens of the Cherokee nation, as they were called in the Holsten treaty, and the Senate of the United States had sanctioned the acts, by which they had risen into a highly civilized state. While refusing to sell their lands, and planting themselves on the treaty guaranty of the Federal government, with covetous and impatient eye, the State of Georgia claimed the right of possession; and extended her laws over her fellow-christians of Moravian, Presbyterian, Baptist and Methodist churches; by which they were brought into a state of degradation and defenselessness like that of slavery, and declared to be incapable of being witnesses or parties in a court of justice. They were made outlaws upon their own lands, and allowed but the privilege of choosing between exile and chains.

It may be proper here to enter into details. In 1829 the Cherokees possessed a regularly organized civil government, and a written language. The latter was an invention of a native uninstructed Cherokee. Unlike to any that ever existed, it was yet so complete, that adults, by the use of it, could learn to read their native tongue in ten, five, and even three days. The mass of the people, in their dress, houses, furniture, agriculture, implements, manner of cultivating the soil, raising stock, providing for their families, and in their estimate of the value of an education, did not suffer by a comparison with the whites in the surrounding settlements. The great body of the people had externally embraced the christian religion. Intemperance, the bane of the Indian as well as of the white man, had been checked. The laws of the nation rigorously excluded intoxicating liquors from all public assemblies. In this respect they set a noble and lofty example, worthy of being imitated by our Congress and State Legislatures. Numerous and efficient societies for the promotion of temperance, had been organized, and prosperity smiled upon them. But, in two years afterward, in spite of all their improvements, by the action of Georgia, the nation had been thrown into a distracted state; their government prostrated; their council forbidden to assemble; their laws declared null and void; their magistrates prohibited, under severe penalties, from enforcing them; intoxicating liquors introduced without restraint; the country traversed with armed troops; their property plundered; their persons arrested and imprisoned; their land,—known to be theirs by ancestral and immemorial possession, and guaranteed to them by numerous and perfectly explicit treaties,—claimed by others; and they themselves threatened with immediate ejectment!

The missionaries, at four stations lying within the territory claimed by Georgia, were served with copies of a law, requiring an oath of allegiance to that State within a limited period, or imprisonment for four years in the penitentiary for refusal. Important civil, moral, and religious rights, and personal liberties, were thus invaded and violated. The missionaries could not, in good conscience, take the oath; for it would be an abandonment of the

Indians' rights secured by treaty with the Federal government, and an admission that Georgia was right.

A detachment of the Georgia guard, consisting of twenty-six men, armed and mounted, proceeded to each of the four missionary stations, and arrested three of the missionaries found there. They were, however, set free, by the Judge of the Superior Court of Gwinnet county, on the ground that they were under the patronage of the United States government, and were in such sense its agents, that the laws of Georgia did not apply to them. The Governor of Georgia corresponded with the President of the United States on the subject. The result was, that the latter did not consider the missionaries as in any sense agents of the government. Thereupon the missionaries were ordered, within ten days, to remove out of the State, or take the required oath.

Several of the missionaries, Messrs. Buttrick, Proctor, and Thompson, thought it expedient to remove, with their families. Mr. Thompson was subsequently arrested, and treated in the most brutal manner, for visiting his station. Mr. Worcester and Dr. Butler were arrested, and subjected to cruelties and indignities, such as savages themselves would scarcely inflict upon their captives. They were tried; and along with eight other white men, one a missionary of the Methodist Episcopal church, were sentenced to four years' hard labor in the penitentiary. On their arrival at the door of the prison, they were all offered a pardon and release, on condition, of their removing from the Indian territory claimed by the State of Georgia, or of taking the oath of allegiance to its laws. All but two of them accepted these humiliating terms. Mr. Worcester and Dr. Butler, feeling that obedience to such laws would be treason against God, conceded nothing, and were committed to the penitentiary.

The matter was brought before the Supreme Court of the United States, on a writ of error. Having been ably argued by Messrs. Wirt and Sergeant, Chief Justice Marshall pronounced his decision. He reviewed the whole subject of the Indian titles, the treaties made with the Indians, and the laws of Georgia, which extended the jurisdiction of the State over the Cherokee country. The laws of Georgia were pronounced repugnant to the constitution, the treaties, and the laws of the United States. The mandate of the Supreme Court was instantly issued, reversing and annulling the judgment of the Superior Court of Georgia, and ordering all proceedings in the indictment against the prisoners forever to cease, declaring the prisoners to be thereby dismissed. The Superior Court of Georgia refused to obey the mandate, or discharge the prisoners. The authority of the Supreme Court of the United States thus set at defiance, the country became excited, especially the religious and order-loving, law-abiding citizens.

There existed a difference of opinion, if not a contest for the ultimate authority, between the President and the Chief Justice of the Supreme Court of the United States. The latter, it was known, would require a military enforcement. The counsel of the imprisoned missionaries prepared a memorial to the former, praying for the interposition of his authority to enforce the decision of the court. The missionaries gave notice of their intention to move the Supreme Court for a further process. They had been sustained by the public sentiment of the christian community, especially at the North, as well as by their official advisers and directors in the work of missions, the prudential Committee of the Amerian Board of Conference for Foreign Missions. It was thought by many to be a proper juncture and opportunity to settle the question, whether the Supreme Court or the President of the United States, the Judiciary or Executive, possessed the ultimate authority; and especially, amid the rising excitement of South Carolina nullification, to put to the test the authority of the treaties, laws, and Constitution of the United States, and the strength and integrity of the Federal government and Union. Georgia had bid defiance to the authority of the Supreme Court; and, by a corrupting policy,—appealing to human cupidity, for the distribution among her citizens, by lottery, 140 acres each, of the whole Cherokee country lying within her chartered limits, previously surveyed and divided into lots for that purpose,—had rendered her legislation and defiant claims popular.

We shall not further trespass on your time here, to enter into other details of this disgraceful history. It may suffice to say, that upon various consultations it was thought inexpedient—we say not by whom, but not by the imprisoned missionaries themselves or their counsel,—to present their memorial to the President for the enforcement of the decision of the court. My personal reminiscences here of matters learned from Dr. Butler himself—who spent several days in my house as my honored guest, soon after his removal from the penitentiary—are as painful at this distant day, as they were in their commencement, having been subversive of the respectful consideration previously entertained for the patriotic and religious men, whose timidity, called and mistaken for prudence, led them to change the counsel and policy, in accordance with which the missionaries had all along acted in the assertion of right and liberty.

It was well understood that the Supreme Court of the United States would sustain its own decision, and demand the support of the executive authority of the government, by military force if necessary. And it was also as well understood, that the President was not inclined to enforce it. To prosecute the case would lead to a collision of the authorities, and the result was thought doubtful. The missionaries were, therefore, often and earnestly counseled to desist from their attempt to obtain release by a military enforcement of the decision of the Supreme Court. They were assured of an unconditional release in case they would do so. But they refused. They spurned a pardon. They would not escape from the prison, even when the doors were thrown open for them. Persons in the confidence of the Governor of Georgia visited them, and earnestly solicited them to desist from the

prosecution. They made "no solicitation, no over-
ture, no compromise" whatever.

Two members elect of Congress visited them,
and told them officially from the Governor, that
they would be discharged without concession, without condition, or even without application to the
Governor. To desist from the prosecution of the
suit, they were assured, would end the whole matter.
It would relieve the Court, the President, the esti-
mable Governor, the State of Georgia, and the
country. Their friends and counselors in Boston,
no longer advised to firmness in the prosecution.
The prisoners' counsel dropped all proceedings.
Messrs. Worcester and Butler were set at liberty by
proclamation from the Governor of Georgia, directed
to the keeper of the penitentiary; and the Governor's
carriage, it was currently reported, was in waiting
for them when they left the prison. They immediately returned to the stations which they had
respectively occupied in the Cherokee country, and
resumed their missionary labors.

The country and its authorities, had passed a
crisis. But the fate of the Cherokee was sealed.
The robbery and violence of Georgia had proved
victorious; and the Supreme Court of the United
States then received the first blow which struck
it from its lofty position as the ultimate authority,—
the grand balance wheel and regulating power in
our government—and rendered it, as many fear,
rather the dim reflector of the policy of the executive, than the independent interpreter of the constitution. Be that as it may, it has suffered great

loss in public confidence and estimation at the North. The executive policy triumphed over right. By means of a treaty obtained from unauthorized and unfaithful representatives of the Cherokee people, through the aid of intoxicating drinks—a plan for removing the Indians, pronounced benevolent, was carried out. The Cherokees were denationalized; and scenes of pillage, plunder, and mortality, shocking to relate, consummated and aggravated the guilt of a violated treaty. The inspired lawgiver of the Jewish nation proclaimed:

"Cursed be he that removeth his neighbor's landmark, and all the people shall say amen.

"Cursed be he that maketh the blind to wander out of the way, and all the people shall say amen.

"Cursed be he that perverteth the judgment of the stranger, fatherless, and widow, and all the people shall say amen."

The landmarks were removed; the blind and helpless were led out of the way and banished from their habitations and homes, by violence; judgment was perverted; Washington dishonored; the Senate of the United States stultified; and treaty documents, preserved in the treasuries of State, were torn from our statute books, and scattered to the winds.

It was then declared by many, and we felt at the time, no hesitation in saying, that the nation had incurred the guilt of violated treaties; and that a bitter roll of "mourning, and lamentation, and woe," would be unfolded to the people of the United States. It has been written in characters indelible.

Every where may be met the black traces of that fatal seal, which then was stamped upon the hitherto stainless escutcheon of our country. The natural and legitimate influence of that example has demoralized the land. "We have hatched cockatrice's eggs, and woven the spider's web. He that hath eaten of the eggs has died, and that which was crushed hath broken out into a viper." We have sowed the wind and are reaping the whirlwind. God has withdrawn from us the protection of moral restraint, once mighty to protect and preserve. It is not at all strange, that treaties and compacts have lost their sacredness in the eyes of multitudes; that the constitution has ceased to be a bond of union; that States have repudiated their obligations; that oaths of office are disregarded; that plighted faith is violated; that honor and honesty need the strong power of the law to support them; that the law itself has lost its commanding majesty; that fraud, and peculation, and corruption can be traced from the councils of aldermen to the cabinet of the chief magistrate; and that sober-minded, virtuous citizens stand amazed, and are ready to ask in the language of holy writ, "when the Son of man cometh shall he find faith on the earth?"

The success of Georgia emboldened Alabama; South Carolina soon after proclaimed nullification. The Supreme Court of the United States has lost much of its power and respect. The chief executive having claimed to interpret the constitution for himself, the spirit of lawlessness has grown apace;

3A

and contempt for institutions, usages, and compacts, time-honored and fraught with benefits, now gives indication that the very joints and sinews of society have been *dislocated and strained.* The strifes and agitation of slavery have not only turned the halls of Congress, often, into a bear-garden, and given exhibitions of brutal violence; but churches have repudiated compacts, and set aside at will all corporate rights. The General Assembly of the Presbyterian church, by one party act, through a packed majority, ignored the covenant of the fathers; rode violently over the constitution; set at naught all the obligations of discipline; and by one summary exscinding act, cut off four synods, with their presbyteries and congregations, and 60,000 members; seized and held the property and possessions, wrested from those who had largely contributed it; and hold it still, though every decision of courts, where trials have been conducted, have recognized or affirmed the legal and constitutional body, to be that with which they ecclesiastically broke faith, and refuse to resume it.

Other ecclesiastical bodies have been rent also. And our own New School Presbyterian Assembly, in reaching over a synod to express a judgment of censure bearing on a Presbytery, without trial or constitutional right, gave occasion and pretext, on the ground of violated faith, for the separation of southern brethren from us, and the organization of a new body.

The traces of this thing are interminable. Its roots strike deep into every part of society. Its developments and growths, we regard as even worse, and far more fatal to the welfare and safety of this Union, than slavery itself, however pestiferous that may be, and blighting to the prosperity of the States that cherish it. It is this readiness to violate compacts, to set aside constitutional law, to repudiate the obligations of good faith, that we regard the most alarming feature of the times. If not cured or corrected, it must prove the inevitable precursor of our ruin. How it is to be remedied, God only knows. Our only hope is in the effusion of the Holy Spirit, which the Lord Jesus Christ has power to grant, by which to turn the heart of this people back again unto Him. This can give wisdom, and firmness, and prudence, and zeal, and fidelity in our rulers; and, reforming the masses, counteract the influence of corrupt examples and demoralizing ambitions. God grant a baptism of this Spirit to the whole nation, to bring us to repentance, and teach us to keep His statutes, and commandments, and ordinances, as the means of our happiness and security.

II. A word or two, in conclusion, as to the grounds on which we may venture to pray in hope for this, as the means of preserving us a united people.

First, there is the boundless and amazing grace and compassion of God, toward those that have no just claim upon Him. How often did He exhibit and exercise that grace and compassion, in the history of ungrateful and perfidious Israel! "Their heart was not right with Him, neither were

they steadfast in His covenant; but He being full
of compassion, forgave their iniquity and destroyed
them not: yea, many a time turned He His anger
away, and did not stir up all His wrath; for He
remembered they were but flesh; a wind that passeth away and cometh not again." It is as true
in the past history of our own beloved country.
Signal have been His interpositions, and abounding
His compassions toward us as a nation. Oh, what
a flood of grateful recollections does the history of
this people bear along with it, from before the days
of our revolutionary sires to the present. "He
hath done great things for us whereof we have
reason to be glad."

When we look at the manifestation of His own
amazing grace and compassion, His own lofty and
glorious excellence, as the God "who delighteth in
mercy," why should we despair? The fountain
of His overflowing love is not exhausted. He is
loath to execute His judgments in wrath. His
own loving heart, His abounding compassions, well
up, in exhaustless exuberant overflowings. What
may we not hope and pray for from Him, whose
name and nature is Love? Could the eyes and
heart of this people but be fixed on God Himself, as
He comes to us in Christ, filled with the Spirit,
without measure, all would yet be well. With such
a God, and such a Saviour, and such a Spirit, to
appeal to, let us drive away our unbelieving, guilty
fears, and draw near with the full assurance of
faith as we pray: "Oh remember not against us
former iniquities. Let Thy tender mercies speedily

prevent us—at this very moment rise before us, and keep us from sinking utterly—for we are brought very low. Help us, O God of our salvation, for the glory of Thy name, and deliver us, and purge away our sins for Thy name's sake."

This forms the second ground of hope, the conscious exercise of penitence in an appeal to God for His help, that we may be delivered, and our sins be purged from us. Without this, all prayer to Him will prove unavailing. If we fast and pray for party strife and debate, and to smite with the fist of wickedness, or practice oppression and deceit, the Lord will not hear us. God knows our hearts; and He has said, "if we regard iniquity in our hearts He will not hear us." But He says, "Let the wicked forsake his way, and the unrighteous man his thoughts; and let him return unto the Lord, and He will have mercy upon him; and to our God, for He will abundantly pardon." If this people, this day, though not universally, yet in sufficient numbers to give to God a public reason for the exercise of His clemency and compassion through Christ, shall truly and heartily renounce their sins, and confess and turn away from those things which have displeased Him, He will forgive, and not destroy us. Let each and every one of us, then, as we love our souls, our country, and our God, renounce and confess to Him, our own personal sins and those of the nation, in so far as we have knowledge and participation of them.

We shall thus find that we can draw near to God with renewed confidence and enlarged expectations, and be in a better frame and spirit to influence and lead from error and sin, our neighbors and friends who practice what we judge to be wrong.

It is the glory of God to forgive: all the lustre of His name, all the excellencies of His character display themselves here. He has said, "I, even I, am He that blotteth out thy transgressions, and will not remember thy sins any more for My name's sake; put Me in remembrance; declare thou that thou mayest be justified." If the hearts of the people to any extent, will only believe this, so that with conscious exercise of repentance for all past sins, they come to God, and throw themselves and this nation upon His grace and compassion, His very name and nature—the infinite, adorable excellencies of His character, as they reveal themselves in the blessed Redeemer, who is the name of God—will form the strong plea, the prevailing argument, so that with Jeremiah, the weeping prophet, we may confidently plead for our country as he did for his. "We acknowledge, O Lord, our wickedness, and the iniquity of our fathers, for we have sinned against Thee. Do not abhor us, for Thy name's sake; do not disgrace the throne of Thy glory."

Finally, we may take occasion, from the terrible character of the evils deprecated, to become importunate with God. Moses prayed with fervor, and fell down forty days and nights before the Lord, in prayer, that He would not destroy the nation. Dissolution and destruction are the evils that threaten us. If God gives not repentance to put away voluntarily, the evils of slavery, and those it has developed, He will, as He ever has done, interfere by His judgments to do it. Who can contemplate such a procedure of His providence, without shuddering? It is no subject for flippant and angry debates or discussions and bitter revilings. It would seem that He hath smitten already with blindness, and that those more immediately periled, see not the disaster and ruin they are courting by the attitude they have assumed. If gradual emancipation is refused—as past history in every country has shown—insurrection, murder, conflagration, rapine, violence, will do it. Secession and separation will invite to these things, and, ere the crisis comes, who can tell how many hearts shall bleed, and homes be rendered desolate, by the horrors of civil war? It may be, that God shall leave us to folly and madness, to break the pillar of our constitution, shake down upon our heads the great and glorious temple of our confederacy, raised by the wisdom, and consecrated by the prayers of our sires of olden days, and involve ourselves in its ruins. But ere that day comes, while yet there is hope of averting the avenging stroke of heaven's wrath, it behooves every christian and patriot to try what conciliation, repentance, fervent prayer, intercession with God, can accomplish. We tremble in view of His judgments and wrath, for we are guilty. But knowing His great compassion, still let us pray, "O Lord, though our enemies testify against us, do Thou, for Thy name's sake spare, and give not Thy heritage to reproach. Oh, the hope of Israel, and the Saviour thereof in time of trouble, why shouldst thou be as a stranger in the land, and as a wayfaring man that turneth aside to tarry for a night? Why shouldst thou be as a man astonished; as a mighty man that cannot save? Yet Thou, O Lord, art in the midst of us, and we are called by Thy name, LEAVE US NOT!"